T0159871

CLASSIC MOMENTS FROM

Little Women

LOUISA MAY ALCOTT

Published by Ice House Books

Copyright © 2019 Ice House Books
Illustrations by Jocelyn Kao
Original text by Louisa May Alcott

Ice House Books is an imprint of Half Moon Bay Limited
The Ice House, 124 Walcot Street, Bath, BA1 5BG
www.icehousebooks.co.uk

This is a celebration of the novel and not intended as a direct
replica of the original text. Excerpts have been selected and some
text has been omitted to create a collection of well-loved scenes.

ISBN 978-1-912867-34-9

Printed in China

CLASSIC MOMENTS FROM

Little Women

LOUISA MAY ALCOTT

ICE HOUSE BOOKS

From Chapter I

"Christmas won't be Christmas without any presents," grumbled Jo, lying on the rug.

"It's so dreadful to be poor!"

sighed Meg, looking down at her old dress.

"I don't think it's fair for some girls to have lots of pretty things, and other girls nothing at all," added little Amy, with an injured sniff.

"We've got father and mother and each other, anyhow," said Beth, contentedly, from her corner.

The four young faces on which the firelight shone brightened at the cheerful words, but darkened again as Jo said sadly,—

"We haven't got father, and shall not have him for a long time." She didn't say "perhaps never," but each silently added it, thinking of father far away, where the fighting was.

Nobody spoke for a minute; then Meg said in an altered tone,—

"You know the reason mother proposed not having any presents this Christmas, was because it's going to be a hard winter for every one; and she thinks we ought not to spend money for pleasure, when our men are suffering so in the army."

"But I don't think the little we should spend would do any good. We've each got a dollar, and the army wouldn't be much helped by our giving that. I agree not to expect anything from mother or you, but I do want to buy Undine and Sintram for myself; I've wanted it so long," said Jo, who was a bookworm.

[...]

Margaret, the eldest of the four, was sixteen and very pretty, being plump and fair, with large eyes, plenty of soft brown hair, and a sweet mouth. Fifteen-year old Jo was very tall. She had a decided mouth, a comical nose, and sharp gray eyes, which appeared to see everything. Her long, thick hair was her one beauty; but it was usually bundled into a net. Round shoulders had Jo, and the uncomfortable appearance of a girl who was ...

... *rapidly shooting up into a woman, and didn't like it.*

Elizabeth—or Beth, as everyone called her—was a rosy, smooth-haired, bright-eyed girl of thirteen, with a shy manner, a timid voice, and a peaceful expression, which was seldom disturbed. Amy, though the youngest, was a most important person, in her own opinion at least. A regular snow maiden with blue eyes, and yellow hair curling on her shoulders.

From Chapter V

On the other side was a stately stone mansion.

To Jo's lively fancy this fine house seemed a kind of enchanted palace, full of splendors and delights, which no one enjoyed. She had long wanted to behold these hidden glories, and to know the "Laurence boy," who looked as if he would like to be known, if he only knew how to begin.

"There he is," thought Jo; "poor boy! all alone, and sick, this dismal day! I'll toss up a snow-ball, and make him look out, and then say a kind word to him."

Up went a handful of soft snow, and the head turned at once, showing a face which lost its listless look in a minute, as the big eyes brightened, and the mouth began to smile.

"How do you do? Are you sick?"

Laurie opened the window and croaked out as hoarsely as a raven,—

"Better, thank you. I've had a horrid cold, and been shut up a week."

"I'm sorry. What do you amuse yourself with?"

"Nothing; it's as dull as tombs up here."

"Can't somebody read to you?"

"Grandpa does, sometimes; but my books don't interest him, and I hate to ask Brooke all the time."

"Isn't there some nice girl who'd read and amuse you? Girls are quiet, and like to play nurse."

"Don't know any."

"You know me," began Jo, then laughed, and stopped.

"So I do! Will you come, please?" cried Laurie.

"I'm not quiet and nice; but I'll come."

From Chapter VIII

"Girls, where are you going?" asked Amy, finding Jo and Meg getting ready to go out.

"Never mind; little girls shouldn't ask questions," returned Jo sharply.

Turning to Meg, she said coaxingly, "Do tell me! I should think you might let me go, too."

"I can't, dear, because you aren't invited," began Meg; but Jo broke in impatiently, "Now, Meg, be quiet, or you will spoil it all. You can't go, Amy; so don't be a baby, and whine about it."

[...]

The next day Jo made a discovery which produced a tempest. "Has anyone taken my story?"

Meg and Beth said "No," at once, and looked surprised; Amy poked the fire, and said nothing. Jo saw her colour rise, and was down upon her in a minute.

"Amy, you've got it!"

"No, I haven't."

"That's a fib!" cried Jo.

"Scold as much as you like, you'll never get your silly old story again," cried Amy, getting excited in her turn.

"Why not?"

"I burnt it up."

"What! my little book I was so fond of, and worked over, and meant to finish before father got home? Have you really burnt it?" said Jo.

"Yes, I did! I told you I'd make you pay for being so cross yesterday, and I have, so—"

"You wicked, wicked girl! I never can write it again, and I'll never forgive you as long as I live."

[...]

As Laurie turned the bend, he shouted back,—

"Keep near the shore; it isn't safe in the middle."

Jo heard, but Amy was just struggling to her feet, and did not catch a word. Jo glanced over her shoulder, and the little demon she was harbouring said in her ear,—

"No matter whether she heard or not ...

... let her take care of herself."

Laurie had vanished round the bend; Jo was just at the turn, and Amy, far behind, striking out toward the smoother ice in the middle of the river. For a minute Jo stood still, with a strange feeling at her heart; then she resolved to go on, but something held and turned her round, just in time to see Amy throw up her hands and go down, with the sudden crash of rotten ice, the splash of water, and a cry that made Jo's heart stand still with fear.

From Chapter XV

A sharp ring interrupted Mrs. March, and a minute after Hannah came in with a letter.

"It's one of them horrid telegraph things, mum."

At the word "telegraph," Mrs. March snatched it, read the two lines it contained, and dropped back into her chair as white as if the little paper had sent a bullet to her heart. Laurie dashed down stairs for water, while Meg and Hannah supported her, and Jo read aloud, in a frightened voice,—

"MRS. MARCH:

"Your husband is very ill. Come at once.

"S. HALE,

"Blank Hospital, Washington."

How still the room was as they listened breathlessly! how strangely the day darkened outside! and now suddenly the whole world seemed to change, as the girls gathered about their mother, feeling as if all the happiness and support of their lives ...

... was about to be taken from them.

Mrs. March was herself again directly; read the message over, and stretched out her arms to her daughters, saying, in a tone they never forgot, "I shall go at once, but it may be too late; oh, children, children! help me to bear it!"

They tried to be calm, poor things, as their mother sat up, looking pale, but steady, and put away her grief to think and plan for them.

"Where's Laurie?" she asked presently. "Send a telegram saying I will come at once. The next train goes early in the morning; I'll take that."

UNION COMPANY.

MRS. MARCH:
Your husband is very ill.
Come at once.
S. HALE,
Blank Hospital,
Washington.

[...]

Jo came walking in with a very queer expression of countenance, which puzzled the family as much as did the roll of bills she laid before her mother, saying, with a little choke in her voice, "That's my contribution towards making father comfortable, and bringing him home!"

"My dear, where did you get it! Twenty-five dollars! Jo, I hope you haven't done anything rash?"

"No, it's mine honestly; I didn't beg, borrow, nor steal it. I earned it; and I don't think you'll blame me, for I only sold what was my own."

As she spoke, Jo took off her bonnet, and a general outcry arose ...

... *for all her abundant hair was cut short.*

"Your hair! Your beautiful hair!" "Oh, Jo, how could you? Your one beauty." "My dear girl, there was no need of this." "She don't look like my Jo any more, but I love her dearly for it!"

From Chapter XVIII

The first of December was a wintry day indeed to them, for a bitter wind blew, snow fell fast, and the year seemed getting ready for its death. When Dr. Bangs came that morning, he looked long at Beth, held the hot hand in both his own a minute, and laid it gently down, saying, in a low tone, to Hannah,—

"If Mrs. March can leave her husband, she'd better be sent for."

Hannah nodded without speaking, for her lips twitched nervously; Meg dropped down into a chair, and Jo, after standing with a pale face for a minute, ran to the parlor, snatched up the telegram, and, throwing on her things, rushed out into the storm. She was soon back, and, while noiselessly taking off her cloak, Laurie came in with a letter, saying that Mr. March was mending again. Jo read it thankfully, but the heavy weight did not seem lifted off her heart.

"Beth is my conscience, and I can't give her up; I can't! I can't!"

Down went Jo's face into the wet handkerchief, and she cried despairingly; for she had kept up bravely till now, and never shed a tear. Laurie drew his hand across his eyes. Presently, as Jo's sobs quieted, he said, hopefully, "I don't think she will die; she's so good, and we all love her so much, I don't believe God will take her away yet."

"The good and dear people always do die," groaned Jo, but she stopped crying, for her friend's words cheered her up, in spite of her own doubts and fears.

From Chapter XXII

Several days of unusually mild weather fitly ushered in a splendid Christmas-day. Mr. March wrote that he should soon be with them; then Beth felt uncommonly well that morning. Laurie opened the parlour door, and popped his head in quietly.

"Here's another Christmas present for the March family."

In his place appeared a tall man. Mr. March became invisible in the embrace of four pairs of loving arms. Mrs. March was the first to recover herself, and held up her hand with a warning, "Hush! remember Beth!"

But it was too late; the study door flew open and Beth ran straight into her father's arms. Never mind what happened just after that; for the full hearts overflowed, washing away the bitterness of the past, and leaving only the sweetness of the present.

From Chapter XXVII

Fortune suddenly smiled upon Jo, and dropped a good-luck penny in her path.

She was prevailed upon to escort Miss Crocker to a lecture, and in return for her virtue was rewarded with an idea.

On her right, her only neighbour was a studious-looking lad absorbed in a newspaper.

It was a pictorial sheet, and Jo examined the work of art nearest her. Pausing to turn a page, the lad saw her looking, and offered half his paper, saying, bluntly, "Want to read it? That's a first-rate story."

Jo accepted it with a smile.

"Prime, isn't it?" asked the boy, as her eye went down the last paragraph of her portion. "She makes a good living out of such stories, they say."

"Do you say she makes a good living out of stories like this?" and Jo looked more respectfully at the agitated group and thickly-sprinkled exclamation points that adorned the page.

"Guess she does! she knows just what folks like, and gets paid well for writing it."

She said nothing of her plan at home.

The manuscript was privately despatched, accompanied by a note.

Six weeks is a long time to wait, and a still longer time for a girl to keep a secret; but Jo did both, and was just beginning to give up all hope of ever seeing her manuscript again, when a letter arrived which almost took her breath away; for, on opening it, a check for a hundred dollars fell into her lap.

From Chapter XXXII

"You asked me the other day what my wishes were. I'll tell you one of them, Marmee," Jo began, as they sat alone together. "I want to go away somewhere this winter."

"Why, Jo?"

With her eyes on her work, Jo answered soberly, "I want something new; I feel restless. I brood too much over my own small affairs, and need stirring up, so as I can be spared this winter I'd like to hop a little way and try my wings."

"Where will you hop?"

"To New York. You know Mrs. Kirke wrote to you for some respectable young person to teach her children and sew. It's rather hard to find just the thing, but I think I should suit if I tried."

"Are these your only reasons for this sudden fancy?"

"No, mother."

"May I know the others?"

Jo looked up and Jo looked down, then said slowly, with sudden colour in her cheeks, "It may be vain and wrong to say it, but—

... I'm afraid—Laurie is getting too fond of me."

"Then you don't care for him in the way it is evident he begins to care for you?"

"Mercy, no! I love the dear boy as I always have, and am immensely proud of him; but as for anything more, it's out of the question."

[...]

When Laurie said "Good-by," he whispered, significantly, "It won't do a bit of good, Jo. My eye is on you; so mind what you do, or I'll come and bring you home."

From Chapter XXXIV

Though very happy in the social atmosphere about her, Jo still found time for literary labours.

She took to writing sensation stories and told no one, but concocted a "thrilling tale," and boldly carried it herself to Mr. Dashwood, editor of the "Weekly Volcano."

[...]

I don't know whether the study of Shakespeare helped her to read character, or the natural instinct of a woman for what was honest, brave and strong; but while endowing her imaginary heroes with every perfection under the sun ...

... Jo was discovering a live hero, who interested her in spite of many human imperfections.

Mr. Bhaer had advised her to study simple, true, and lovely characters, as good training for a writer; Jo took him at his word,—for she coolly turned round and studied him.

[...]

Another and a better gift than intellect was shown her in a most unexpected manner. Miss Norton had the *entrée* into literary society. She took Jo and Mr. Bhaer with her, one night, to a select symposium, held in honour of several celebrities.

Before the evening was half over, Jo felt so completely *désillusionnée*, that she sat down in a corner, to recover herself. Mr. Bhaer soon joined her and presently several of the philosophers came ambling up to hold an intellectual tournament in the recess.

Jo looked round to see how the Professor liked it, and found him looking at her with the grimmest expression she had ever seen him wear.

He bore it as long as he could; but when he was appealed to for an opinion, he blazed up with honest indignation, and defended religion with all the eloquence of truth.

She remembered this scene, and gave the Professor her heartiest respect.

[...]

It was a pleasant winter and a long one, for Jo did not leave Mrs. Kirke till June. Every one seemed sorry when the time came; the children were inconsolable, and Mr. Bhaer's hair stuck up all over his head—for he always rumpled it wildly when disturbed in mind.

She was going early, so she bade them all good-by over night; and when his turn came, she said, warmly,—

"Now, sir, you won't forget to come and see us, if you ever travel our way, will you? I'll never forgive you, if you do, for I want them all to know my friend."

"Do you? Shall I come?" he asked, looking down at her with an eager expression, which she did not see.

"Yes, come next month; Laurie graduates then, and you'd enjoy Commencement as something new."

"That is your best friend, of whom you speak?" he said, in an altered tone.

"Yes, my boy Teddy; I'm very proud of him, and should like you to see him."

Jo looked up, then, quite unconscious of anything but her own pleasure. Something in Mr. Bhaer's face suddenly recalled the fact that she might find Laurie more than a best friend, and she involuntarily began to blush.

[...]

Early as it was, he was at the station, next morning, to see Jo off; and, thanks to him, she began her solitary journey with the pleasant memory of a familiar face smiling its farewell, a bunch of violets to keep her company, and, best of all, the happy thought,—

"Well, the winter's gone, and I've written no books—earned no fortune; but ...

... I've made a friend worth having, and I'll try to keep him all my life."

From Chapter XXXV

"Now, you must have a good, long holiday!"

"I intend to."

Something in Laurie's resolute tone made Jo look up quickly,—

"No, Teddy,—please, don't!"

"I've loved you ever since I've known you, Jo,— couldn't help it, you've been so good to me,—I've tried to show it, but you wouldn't let me."

"I wanted to save you this; I thought you'd understand—" began Jo, finding it a great deal harder than she expected.

"I know you did; but girls are so queer you never know what they mean. They say No, when they mean Yes; and drive a man out of his wits just for the fun of it," returned Laurie.

"I don't. I never wanted to make you care for me so, and I went away to keep you from it if I could."

"I thought so; it was like you, but it was no use. I only loved you all the more, and I worked hard to please you, and I gave up billiards and everything you didn't like, and waited and never complained, for I hoped you'd love me, though I'm not half good enough—" here there was a choke that couldn't be controlled.

"Yes, you are; you're a great deal too good for me, and I'm so grateful to you, and so proud and fond of you, I don't see why

I can't love you as you want me to.

I've tried, but I can't change the feeling, and it would be a lie to say I do when I don't."

From Chapter XXXVI

Jo felt as if a veil had fallen between her heart and Beth's.

"Jo, dear, I'm glad you know it. I've tried to tell you, but I couldn't."

There was no answer except her sister's cheek against her own,—not even tears,—for when most deeply moved Jo did not cry. She was the weaker then, and Beth tried to comfort and sustain her with her arms about her.

"I have a feeling that it never was intended I should live long. I'm not like the rest of you; I never made any plans about what I'd do when I grew up; I never thought of being married, as you all did. I couldn't seem to imagine myself anything but stupid little Beth, trotting about at home, of no use anywhere but there. I never wanted to go away, and the hard part now is the leaving you all.

I'm not afraid, but it seems as if I should be homesick for you even in heaven."

From Chapter XL

"I used to think I couldn't let you go; but I'm learning to feel that I don't lose you; that you'll be more to me than ever,

and death can't part us, though it seems to."

"I know it cannot, and I don't fear it any longer, for I'm sure I shall be your Beth still, to love and help you more than ever. You must take my place, Jo, and be everything to father and mother when I'm gone. They will turn to you—don't fail them; and if it's hard to work alone, remember that I don't forget you, and that you'll be happier in doing that, than writing splendid books, or seeing all the world; for love is the only thing that we can carry with us when we go, and it makes the end so easy."

"I'll try, Beth;" and then and there Jo renounced her old ambition, pledged herself to a new and better one, acknowledging the poverty of other desires, and feeling the blessed solace of a belief in the immortality of love.

So the spring days came and went, the sky grew clearer, the earth greener, the flowers were up fair and early, and the birds came back in time to say good-by to Beth, who, like a tired but trustful child, clung to the hands that had led her all her life, as father and mother guided her tenderly through the valley of the shadow, and gave her up to God.

As Beth had hoped, the "tide went out easily;" and in the dark hour before the dawn, on the bosom where she had drawn her first breath, she quietly drew her last, with no farewell but one loving look and a little sigh.

From Chapter XLI

The sad news met Amy at Vevey. She bore it very well, and quietly submitted to the family decree, that she should not shorten her visit. But her heart was very heavy—she longed to be at home; and every day looked wistfully across the lake, waiting for Laurie to come and comfort her.

At the corner of the wide, low wall, was a seat. She was sitting here that day, thinking of Beth, and wondering why Laurie did not come. She did not hear him cross the court-yard beyond. He stood a minute, looking at her with new eyes.

"Oh, Laurie, Laurie! I knew you'd come to me!"

I think everything was said and settled then; for, as they stood together quite silent for a moment, with the dark head bent down protectingly over the light one, Amy felt that no one could comfort and sustain her so well as Laurie, and Laurie decided that Amy was the only woman in the world who could fill Jo's place, and make him happy.

From Chapter XLIII

Jo had just managed to call up a smile, when there came a sudden knock at the porch door.

She opened it with hospitable haste, and started,—for there stood a stout, bearded gentleman, beaming on her from the darkness like a midnight sun.

"Oh, Mr. Bhaer, I am so glad to see you!"

"And I to see Miss Marsch,—but no, you haf a party—" and the Professor paused as the sound of voices.

"No, we haven't,—only the family. My brother and sister have just come home, and we are all very happy. Come in, and make one of us."

From Chapter XLVI

Jo wondered what he thought of her; but she didn't care, for in a minute she found herself walking away, arm-in-arm with her Professor ...

... feeling as if the sun had suddenly burst out with uncommon brilliancy ...

... that the world was all right again.

"Jo, I haf nothing but much love to gif you; I came to see if you could care for it, and I waited to be sure that I was something more than a friend. Am I? can you make a little place in your heart for old Fritz?" he added, all in one breath.

"Oh yes!" said Jo, and he was quite satisfied, for she folded both hands over his arm, and looked up at him with an expression that plainly showed how happy she would be to walk through life beside him.

From Chapter XLVIII

For a year Jo and her Professor worked and waited, hoped and loved. The second year began rather soberly, for Aunt March died suddenly. But when their first sorrow was over, they found they had cause for rejoicing, for she had left Plumfield to Jo.

There were a great many holidays at Plumfield, and one of the most delightful was the yearly apple-picking,—for then the Marches, Laurences, Brookeses, and Bhaers turned out in full force. Five years after Jo's wedding one of these fruitful festivals occurred.

Touched to the heart, Mrs. March could only stretch out her arms, as if to gather children and grandchildren to herself, and say, "Oh, my girls, however long you may live ...

... I never can wish you a greater happiness than this!"